W9-BYG-334

Jenny's Pennies
A Nantucket Tradition

by Peter Saverine

Illustrations by Bobbi Eggers

This book is dedicated...

To my mother, Jenny, who taught me the value of the penny picked up and the power of positive dreaming. To my wife, Barbara, who has tolerated my "blue sky" philosophy and my children, Lauren, Justin, Megan and Jeffrey, who have waited patiently while their father stooped down to gather the errant penny, and who now look for lucky pennies of their own. Finally, to Kitty Blenko, mother of my college roommate, who handed me my first penny to toss by the Brant Point Lighthouse that guaranteed my many happy returns to the island.

Do you believe in mermaids
and wishes that come true?

Do you believe in lucky days
when someone's watching over you?

I know I saw a mermaid
    when I gazed upon the sea;

A beautiful copper-haired mermaid
    who was smiling back at me.

5

I saw the mermaid holding something shiny in her hand.
Was it beach glass? A starfish? A conch shell?
Or a dollar made of sand?

No, it was a bright new copper penny
that twinkled in her hand.

I know I saw the mermaid
    just past the Brant Point Light;

Out near the rocky jetties
    with the harbor on my right.

I think I'll name her Jenny,
      the mermaid by the jetties.
I think I'll name her Jenny,
      the mermaid with the pennies.

A wave or two rolled over her head
      as she disappeared from sight.
I wonder, where does Jenny go
      until the moon comes out at night?

From the tales of early settlers
 and old whalers with their lore,
I understand what Jenny does
 once boats and ferries leave the shore.

She keeps watch of all the faces
 on the boys and girls for years,
Who toss pennies by the lighthouse
 as they wipe away their tears.

Sad that vacation's almost over
  and to school they'll soon return.

As their Nantucket memories linger,
  for the Grey Lady's hug they'll yearn.

Then Jenny dives to catch each penny
with its wish to come back soon,

And she shares them with her island friends
underneath the 'tucket moon.

Riding on the gentle winds
and waves upon the sand...

Seagulls, seals, and horseshoe crabs
bring Jenny's pennies to the land.

They're scattered by rose cottages of Sconset
and near the general store.

Where sunsets paint the sky over Madaket,
they always leave some more.

You can find them on the Children's Beach,
on Jetties and Surfside, too.

At Cisco and Dionis, and...

...on Main Street quite a few.

24

Jenny's pennies give us hope
  that someday we'll all come back,

To our favorite little island
  that is fondly known as "ACK".

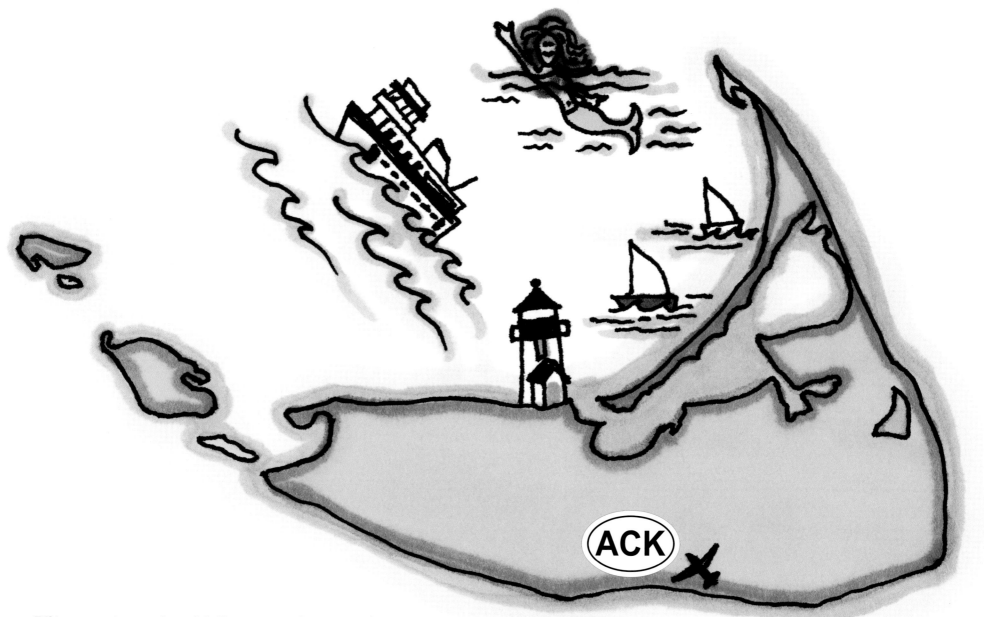

The island of Nantucket, alone out in the sea,

Where life just seems so perfect,
  like how it's supposed to be.

27

So, catch a glimpse out in the Sound
of Jenny's flowing copper hair,

And keep your eyes upon the ground
to find the pennies she left there.

29

Toss Jenny's lucky pennies
by Brant Point as you go 'round,

And it won't be long till once again
you'll cross Nantucket Sound.

Jenny's Pennies
A Nantucket Tradition

Text and illustrations copyright © 2009 by Peter C. Saverine

www.jennyspennies.us

Published by:
Lucky Penny Media, LLC
Southport, CT
www.luckypennymedia.com

All rights reserved. No part of this book may be reproduced, stored in a retrieval system or transmitted, in any form, or by any means, electronic, mechanical, recorded, photocopied, or otherwise without the prior permission of the copyright owner, except by a reviewer who may quote brief passages in a review.

Illustrated by Bobbi Eggers

Special thanks to PCI Group, Stamford, CT for design and printing expertise, and to John and Jane Harwood for their encouragement with this project.

ISBN 978-0-615-28575-7

CPSIA Section 103 (a) Compliant
www.beaconstar.com/ consumer
ID: L0118350. Tracking No.: L2112470-8519

Printed in China

About the Author: Peter Saverine was born and raised in Darien, CT and has lived in Fairfield County with his wife and four children for most of his life. He is a graduate of Amherst College with a BA in Political Science and has spent his career in retail merchandising, marketing, and entrepreneurial ventures. He is a landscape painter, with works represented in gallery locations on Nantucket and along the East Coast. Peter has authored newspaper columns and Jenny's Pennies is his first book.

About the Illustrator: Bobbi Eggers, in her first life as Bobbi John, was an executive creative director in advertising. She worked on national ad campaigns for Coca-Cola, Miller Beer, British Airways, P&G, Revlon and Clairol in NYC, London, Amsterdam and Paris. Bobbi is now a happily married mother of 3 and writes and illustrates for magazines and newspapers, as well as a line of gift products called "SportsMom" and "Chardonnay Girls." Bobbi and her growing family have been vacationing in Nantucket for nearly 20 years and long for it during the winters.